MURDER MOST PUZZLING

MURDER MOST PUZZLING

TWENTY MYSTERIOUS CASES TO SOLVE

STEPHANIE VON REISWITZ

CHRONICLE BOOKS
SAN FRANCISCO

TO CHRIS AND LUCIA.

Library of Congress Cataloging-in-Publication Data
Names: Von Reiswitz, Stephanie, author.
Title: Murder most puzzling : 20 mysterious cases to solve /
by Stephanie von Reiswitz.
Description: San Francisco, California : Chronicle Books, [2020]
Identifiers: LCCN 2018039989 | ISBN 9781452171609 alk. paper
Subjects: LCSH: Picture puzzles. | Detective and mystery stories.
Classification: LCC GV1507.P47 V66 2019 | DDC 793.73—dc23
LC record available at https://lccn.loc.gov/2018039989

Manufactured in China.

Design by Kayla Ferriera.

10 9 8 7 6

Chronicle books and gifts are available at special quantity
discounts to corporations, professional associations, literacy
programs, and other organizations. For details and discount
information, please contact our premiums department at
corporatesales@chroniclebooks.com or at 1-800-759-0190.

Chronicle Books LLC
680 Second Street
San Francisco, California 94107
www.chroniclebooks.com

CONTENTS

INTRODUCTION

Your decision to answer the small ad in the *Gazette* was mainly motivated by your meagre finances, and by the vague promise of excitement. Who hasn't wondered what detectives do all day? And you do enjoy a good brain teaser, after all.

The private detective, Medea Thorne, arranges your formal interview in a dingy bar, and when you encounter her you are surprised by her slight stature. Her gaze, however, is steely, and you suspect she's already worked out your shoe size, your original hair colour, and what you've had for your breakfast—which unlike hers did not include a stiff whisky.

"You'll start tomorrow, if that suits," she announces. "Seeing as you're the only applicant. Not that I didn't expect that. After all, people tend to be intimidated by local celebrities. But I'm glad that you're unfazed."

Of course you won't mention that you've never heard of her. Soon enough, though, you'll discover that she is quite well known in police circles for her irritating knack for being right, and that her rate of success is indeed impressive. It'll take you some time to get used to her brusque and at times abrasive manner, her penchant for dubious establishments, and her over-reliance on you as a taxi service as much as an assistant and secretary.

This book is a record of twenty of your adventures together, during which you've solved murders using lateral thinking, riddled out mathematical puzzles, noticed important clues, located stolen goods, and collected hard evidence to put the perpetrators away. Thanks to Medea Thorne's unfortunate habit of dropping a few suggestive remarks about the crime before swanning off elsewhere, it's down to you to do the leg work time and time again.

THE COLLECTOR

Summoned to the beautiful mansion of one Reginald Audley, we encounter Hislop, his diminutive maid, in a state of shock. "He's been coshed on the head!" she exclaims. "I was just about to dust his study—he's not usually in there at this hour!"

"Why did you ring for us, rather than the police?" Medea Thorne demands.

"I would have, only—" Hislop fidgets with her handkerchief. "Well, he's got a few things in his collection that . . . I thought if you could present the evidence to the police, they wouldn't need to look at his treasures too closely."

"Sounds like the old blighter," Ms. Thorne mutters under her breath, lighting one of her black cigars.

According to the sobbing maid, Reginald Audley was a very exacting man. He only recently acquired a piece that he thought perfectly completed his collection to date, and he invited a number of visitors to celebrate. Hislop last saw him just after lunch, when she brought him the cocktail trolley and two trays of lobster sandwiches. He asked her to answer the door and show his guests to the study before she headed out for her afternoon off. Five guests appeared at more or less the same time.

AMBER AUDLEY. Ms. Audley is Mr. Audley's niece and only living relative. "I imagine she stands to inherit," Hislop wails. "But she can't have killed him! They've always got on so well!"

MELUSINE PARIS. A vaudeville dancer—with live snakes—Paris puts on a silly act in outlandish costumes but is rumored to be patient and ruthless. It's common knowledge that she's extorted money from wealthy admirers before.

HANG YOUNG. An art and antiques dealer who's previously sold Mr. Audley a jade egg but only collects nautical artifacts himself. Young is a very polite man, though he and Audley were fierce rivals at auctions. He said he'd only just arrived back from Hong Kong.

THEOBALD CROOKE. Adventurer, diver, and sea captain. A friendly giant of a man, with a very loud and very dirty laugh, he's the son of the wealthy manufacturer of Crooke's Walking Sticks. Pictures all over his arms, made jokes Hislop wouldn't repeat. "Bit of a rotten apple," Mr. Audley used to chuckle, "but knows his treasure trove." They'd been friends at school.

GREGORY RAMSBOTTOM. Hislop hadn't encountered the novelist before, but she recognized his name from a review in the paper. "Can't be very good books," Hislop says, since the review had been rather scathing. She had found him petulant and hadn't liked his manner—sneering at the stone sphinx by the front door, bragging about his own much grander finds back in Egypt. Mr. Audley, too, had been in Egypt as a young man, until his rather sudden return.

When Hislop returned later in the afternoon, they'd all gone, and the house was quiet.

Having completed the interview, Ms. Thorne proceeds to the Display Room, which contains Audley's large collection.

"One person seems very clearly indicated. Do ring the police," she instructs you. "Let them know what's happened. Of course, they'll have to bring in all five suspects. But tell them whom to arrest first."

What do you say?

PICKLED DELIGHTS

One fine Sunday, Medea Thorne persuades you to drive her to the Annual Perfect Pickled Foods Festival, revealing that she's been invited to act as a celebrity judge. "Pickling brings out the best in almost any food," she announces, pointing at the travel-size jar of pickled garlic in her handbag. When you ask why she needs you to drive, she explains, "Because I'm planning to drink."

You pass a pleasant-enough afternoon throwing coconuts, playing tug-of-war, and nibbling deep-fried pickles. Suddenly, just before the winner of the Grand Pickling Prize is to be announced, there is a commotion in the judges' tent. One of the judges lies dead on the floor.

The victim is Adelaide Bartlett, famous food critic for the *Intrepid Times*. She was known as a busybody who used her column to spread malicious gossip. Someone has dealt her several blows to the head.

Contestants delivered their dishes into the judging tent while the judges finished sampling the Best Brines & Brews. The lady invigilating the entrance never noticed anything, so the attack must've happened very quickly. Now the contestants await their fate in the pavilion, where the murder weapon cannot be found. It's not in the judging tent, either.

You manage to track down Ms. Thorne lying behind a large shrubbery. Shaking her, you tell her about the murder. "That Bartlett woman. Bound to happen," she slurs as she stumbles across the lawn to the judging tent. Glaring first at the display of pickles, then at the contestants in the pavilion, she shrugs and hiccups. "But it's ob-obvious. C-can only've been one of them." She hiccups again. "And you can see w-which. You s— you sort it out." Smiling beatifically, she passes out.

What was the murder weapon? Who did it?

Pictured overleaf, left to right:
ISIDOR GRAIN: pickled walnuts
LILY CRACKNELL: piccalilli
JEANNETTE MARSH: beetroot pickled eggs
LUCY WILKINS: rollmops
LEONARD FANSHAWE: pickled cucumbers
WINIFRED RAYBOURNE: pickled pineapple
CHARLES ARROW: pickled cheese

THE BOATING LAKE

"Oh, nothing much," Inspector Symes says when you and Medea Thorne meet him for coffee. "Just this latest murder. Strange case, a body pulled out of the Oakes Park boating lake two weeks ago. A man name of Bertram Shingle, an estate agent and local history buff who'd previously been accused of blackmailing a client, though the charges were dropped. Drowned as well as stabbed multiple times, it seems. The murder weapon can't quite be identified as yet. In fact, the lacerations seem to vary.

"Well, at first we were stumped, to be honest. Nothing much to go on at all. Shingle seemed a diligent type, well-enough liked, considering his profession. According to Mr. Pips, his secretary, he'd been flashing the cash lately, wore new suits, talked about expanding his office. But Pips couldn't connect this to any particularly lucrative new cases.

"It was a piece of luck when the photographer turned up. He'd taken a picture of a group in outlandish attire on the boating lake. Saw the notice in the paper, recognized Shingle.

"Mr. Pips identified the group in the photo as former members of the Aesthetes Society Shingle belonged to at university. Shingle had only recently got reacquainted with them. Maybe he'd started spending so much to compete; apparently, they've got a thing for fancy clothes. Actually, I've got an older picture here. See what you think.

"This is what we know about them:

"Iona Partridge, a sword swallower of some renown. Currently the star turn at the Nonchalance Cabaret Club, having left her previous engagement under somewhat of a cloud. Seems to enjoy the company of petty criminals.

"Helen Garnett, knife thrower and Ms. Partridge's cousin. They work at the same establishment. Joined her cousin after she was suddenly dismissed from the traveling circus. Rumors abound about what happened, none of them pleasant in the least.

"Terrence Carlisle, a local butcher. Apparently an amiable man. It seems his wife was frequently mentioned in Shingle's appointment book.

"Tadhg O'Brien, a thespian currently playing Frederic in *The Pirates of Penzance*. Fancies himself an outstanding actor, a view not generally shared, as he drinks heavily and is prone to blackouts. He's said to indulge in certain unsavory pleasures, though no one would specify what these are.

"Carlotta Ribbons, a former fencing champion who now makes her money teaching fencing classes. Plenty of stories about her fierce professional jealousy and rather violent temper. She's alleged to have incapacitated more than one opponent by dubious means, though nothing was ever proved."

Ms. Thorne says, "Oh, we won't need to speak to them. Just study the photograph from the lake carefully. It's plain as day who did it."

What does she mean?

Pictured overleaf, left to right:
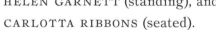
BERTRAM SHINGLE (with champagne), TERRENCE CARLISLE (facing away),
IONA PARTRIDGE (holding an oar), TADHG O'BRIEN (in the blue hat),
HELEN GARNETT (standing), and
CARLOTTA RIBBONS (seated).

THE CHOCOLATE BOX

Medea Thorne has summoned you to The Chasm, a down-at-heel bistro in a dubious part of town.

"I was having a poached egg and a quick livener, trying to hold on to my will to live, when I saw them." She points at a banquette at the back of the room.

"Lydia Irvin, the actress, and a young man with a pencil mustache, flattering her. He was talking rapidly and forced a box of chocolates on her. No sooner had he sauntered off than her real date arrived."

"Roger Blake, no less, the theater magnate. Didn't like strangers giving her gifts, of course, but seemed to enjoy the chocolates. Partial to crème de menthe, it seems."

About an hour later, Ms. Thorne had rung up Inspector Symes about another case. "And he gave me the news. Blake is dead! Started vomiting in the street, collapsed, heart attack. And Irvin in hospital, violently ill. They're suspecting poison. I wonder if it was atropine . . ."

"I might have recognized the young man, too. In fact, think I know who was behind this. Come along."

Rebecca Blake, star of the stage and several recent pictures, opens the door, sporting huge sunglasses. Ms. Thorne informs her that her husband has passed away.

"Oh. Estranged husband," the woman yawns. "I'm sorry. It's very early for me. I never get up before two o'clock. The theater, you know."

Unimpressed, Ms. Thorne embarks on her line of questioning.

"When did I last see him?" Mrs. Blake smiles sweetly. "Yesterday afternoon. From my window. I see them all the time, him and that Irvin woman. They have lunch at The Chasm. I wouldn't be seen dead in there. There's a cheap hotel down a side street. I suppose they come to this area to avoid meeting anyone they know. He's no idea that I live here now. It's only temporary, anyway, until my next film comes through."

"Keep her talking," Ms. Thorne murmurs quietly. "I'm off to ring Symes. Make sure you preserve all eleven pieces of evidence."

Can you find the evidence she means?

THE HESPERIDES

You're walking home late, after an evening spent staking out a suspicious hairdresser's, when Medea Thorne suggests a stiff drink at one of her favorite bars, The Hesperides.

As you approach the establishment—infamously popular with sailors, debauchees, bohemian types, performance artistes, and other dubious characters—you and Ms. Thorne are almost knocked over by three people careering down the road, hurtling toward the bar, and disappearing within.

You recognize them; they're small-time criminals with whom you've had dealings before.

"Stop! Thieves!" a man cries behind you. He's a silversmith at Haggle & Grouse, the large and very fine jewelry shop that these three reprobates have apparently robbed. "They've only taken the most expensive things in the windows," he explains breathlessly. "A ruby necklace, a pair of emerald earrings, a sapphire ring, and five large diamonds. Stabbed our security man! If he doesn't pull through . . ."

"Go in and apprehend them," Ms. Thorne instructs you in a tone that brooks no argument. "And find the loot while you're at it. They're bound to have hidden it somewhere. I'll have a chat with my old friend Lucre, who owns this place. He'll make sure no one leaves."

THE THREE REPROBATES
hiding in the crowd

THE LOOT:

five very large diamonds

one natural ruby necklace

one pair of emerald earrings

one oval-cut sapphire ring

SWEET DEATH

You arrive at the Scrupulous Candy Company just as the ambulance pulls away.

Inspector Symes greets you. "Thanks for coming. It's not murder this time, only attempted. A child passed out after eating a bag of mixed candy. Unfortunately, Professor Lamprey, the owner of this place, went into hysterics when he realized. He's had to be sedated." Symes points at a man slumped in a chair.

"The poor man. This is an excellent shop," Medea Thorne tells you, "even though I haven't got much of a sweet tooth at all." She goes on to explain that Lamprey is a retired mathematician who believes in getting curious young minds to solve math problems in return for a sweet reward. "Even the order in which the jars are arranged might seem random, but isn't at all." She turns to Symes. "Did he have any idea how it was done? Could he tell which of the sweets might've contained the poison?"

"He was adamant that it could only be one of the jars here on the counter." Symes shrugs. "He thinks that Edward Wode, a former employee, must've added a jar when he came by earlier in the day, apparently specifically to insult the professor. According to Lamprey, Wode fancied himself something of a genius but kept making mistakes. The professor had no choice but to fire him, and now Wode's trying to destroy his livelihood."

"You'd better go and arrest him then, hadn't you?" Ms. Thorne smiles, studying the shelves.

"Of course," Symes says. "They're out looking for him now. But we do need to find out which of these jars has been tampered with and establish the nature of the poison, to help the poor child. Of course, I'm going to have them analyzed, but unfortunately our lab is slow, so I was hoping you could give us a pointer about which of these jars to test first."

Ms. Thorne nods. "Absolutely. One jar is particularly indicated." She turns to you. "Wouldn't you say?"

THE TOPIARY GARDEN

To your great surprise, Medea Thorne announces that the two of you are meeting Inspector Symes in the Municipal Topiary Garden.

"This place has gone to seed a bit, hasn't it?" she says to him when you arrive. "These shapes are terribly dated. The city should get someone new in, a young mover and shaker in the topiary world, inject some fresh ideas."

"They're just sticking to the original design," says Symes. "Clifford Crag, the previous gardener, was apparently an incredible stickler for rules and patterns. Insisted things be done a certain way, and had a violent temper to boot. No one ever dared oppose his strict ideas, even after he disappeared."

"Disappeared?" Ms. Thorne asks, lighting one of her black cigars.

"About a decade ago. Left suddenly, but sent a postcard from San Marino about a month later, urging his staff not to tamper with his garden, not to plant or move anything. So every gardener employed here since has done exactly that—maintained the trees and hedges but changed nothing. They're still living in fear that he might come back any day."

"Why exactly are we here?" Ms. Thorne demands impatiently.

"This is the thing. He isn't coming back. Two days ago, on her deathbed, a certain Mrs. Crackenthorpe confessed to his murder. She was an elderly lady who in her younger days used to help out here." Symes sighs deeply. "She had her niece write it all out and then signed the statement. It says she bashed him on the head, pushed him into a hole, and planted a tree on top. Now the niece wants to know if it's true. We've got to follow it up."

"Right." Ms. Thorne puffs on her cigar. "So you'd like us to tell you where to look for the body?"

Symes shrugs uncomfortably. "It's the kind of thing you know how to work out. We'd rather not dig up the whole garden, you see."

"My assistant is going to work this one out for you." Smirking, Ms. Thorne pats you on the back. "Don't take too long over it. I'll stand you a drink at The Hesperides later."

THE FUNERAL PARTY

"We're trying to keep this very quiet," explains Mr. Finlay, the private secretary. "This funeral is a big society event, and we wouldn't want to besmirch it with a lot of negative press."

"A murder, did you say?" Medea Thorne scans the opulent ballroom. "At a funeral?"

"Mr. Theodopoulos's funeral is currently taking place. As you'll know, he was a man of great wealth, so we're expecting a large number of very important people to attend this particularly lavish wake. Of course, the murder of a member of staff is a terrible tragedy. This is why we've called you, to sort this out at once."

He quietly leads the way into the ballroom, where lies the body of a young man who has been viciously stabbed in the back.

"That's Paul Aphis! The cocktail designer!" Ms. Thorne exclaims. "Where is the murder weapon?"

"There isn't one." The secretary swallows hard. "Unless, that is, the murderer has secreted it about their person."

"The wound looks much too big for that," Ms. Thorne says firmly. "Shouldn't you have informed the police?"

"Mr. Theodopoulos III had many close friends whom the presence of the law would make extremely uncomfortable. Naturally, we will inform the police in due course. Until then, I'd rather not have a murderer in our midst."

You and Ms. Thorne follow Finlay across the ballroom, where he unlocks a side door and lets in a group of disgruntled people. "This wake has been arranged according to Mr. Theodopoulos's express wishes, and with the professional help of these people, each of them an expert in their field."

One by one, he introduces them *(see overleaf, left to right)*. ALBERT DANDELYON, florist; BEATRICE GOODE, caterer; CYRIL DE BEAUFORT, room stylist; DIANA DEE, candle consultant; ENRICO MALLOW, perfumer.

Ms. Thorne inspects them through narrowed eyes while nonchalantly helping herself to champagne at the cocktail bar. "I believe old Aphis would've wanted us to sample this excellent champagne. But yes," she says, "we'll take it from here." Handing you a glass, she murmurs, "Ring Inspector Symes, will you? Tell him to come in plainclothes, explain exactly what happened, and inform him of whom to arrest."

SERIAL MURDER

"An informal meeting, he said," Medea Thorne snorts as you approach Inspector Symes's office. "Tenner says some petty crime's got him stumped."

The inspector looks worn out. Having offered the two of you a seat and a drink, he barely makes any small talk before cutting to the chase. "We've got a nasty spate of murders," he says. "They seem entirely random, though my gut tells me that perhaps they are connected. You know a respectable psychic medium, don't you?"

"A psychic?" Ms. Thorne laughs out loud. "Come now, Symes. Let's have a look at this first."

Symes opens a file and spreads out a number of glossy photographs. "There's something odd about each of these. We've looked at the cases from every angle, but on the face of it . . . "

"Oh yes." Ms. Thorne nods almost at once. "They obviously are connected. And this thing," she points at a small object in one of the photos, "have you followed it up?"

Symes frowns. "The lapel pin? The acronym is SLBF, which might stand for any number of companies. Or perhaps a society?"

"Precisely that. I think it's clear what the other three letters must stand for. And it might even lead you straight to the culprit." She turns to you. "Go on, check the phone book and ring them up, will you?"

What organization do you look for in the phone book?

A HAUNTING

One dark and stormy night, Medea Thorne asks you to drive her to a leafy suburb and stop in front of a large, decrepit mansion. In the gravel driveway beyond the gate, a tall and haughty man is talking to a pallid butler, next to a pile of strange equipment.

"I told her," the butler is saying gravely as you approach. "I told her this would come to no good. All the signs were there, but she refused to heed them!" He whips around and makes a little bow. "Oh, good evening, Ms. Thorne." He greets you with a solemn nod, before dabbing at his eyes.

"Medea Thorne!" the other man exclaims. "I thought you didn't believe in ghosts." Turning to you, he shakes your hand with a radiant smile. "Augustin Artaud. Ghost hunter extraordinaire."

As you introduce yourself, Ms. Thorne questions the butler. "Parker, is Ms. Morengo all right? She wasn't at poker tonight, and it's something she doesn't miss. And she mentioned strange happenings last time we spoke. Odd things going on here. Unexplained occurrences. What's going on?"

"I'm afraid she isn't all right," Parker croaks. "For weeks I urged her to get an exorcist in. Those dreadful noises, every night! Ghosts! Apparitions! Ectoplasm in the laundry room!"

"Well, she did call me," Artaud explains. "But I'm afraid I arrived too late. Gilda Morengo is dead."

"Dead?" Ms. Thorne blanches. "How?"

"Killed by a specter!" Parker wails. "A marble urn was dropped on her head by what must have been a poltergeist! When I found her, hunched over . . . " his voice fails, and shaking his head, he gathers his resolve.

"Where is she?" Ms. Thorne hurries toward the front door, and you follow close behind.

"In the green drawing room!" Parker calls after you. "I'm not staying here for a moment longer."

"You'll have to stay and speak to the police," Artaud says sternly. "But I've often encountered this sort of scenario. We'll call them with my findings as soon as I've conducted a full psychic investigation."

Ms. Thorne stops you on the front steps and instructs you quietly. "I'll find Morengo. In the meantime, see if you can find any evidence of this so-called *ghost*. Artaud might be a beautiful man, but he's a charlatan. I'm sure we'll prove the cause of the hauntings, and the motive and opportunity of the murder, without any psychic equipment at all."

DEATH IN THE FOUNTAIN

Having made a great effort and sporting your best monochromatic finery, you're attending a special black-and-white masked ball in aid of the Starving Artists Relief Fund, at Medea Thorne's particular request.

You're intrigued to find that the black-and-white theme extends from the elaborate décor to the cocktails and canapés, and even to the band's instruments.

When there's a sudden shriek and panicked shouts of "Help!" and "Murder!," Ms. Thorne merely rolls her eyes. "Not this again. Can't I attend a single ball without someone getting bumped off?"

Having instructed a footman to lock the doors, she leads the way toward the commotion. A body is slumped in the marble basin of the ink fountain.

Ms. Thorne examines the body carefully. "She's been stabbed in the back of the neck," she quietly explains, "with what appears to have been some sort of skewer, probably no thicker than a chopstick."

No one appears to have noticed a struggle, though once her mask is removed, the victim is identified as one Violetta Sharp. When you ask who might have had a grudge against her, Ms. Thorne stops you. "There is so much jealousy amongst this lot," she points out. "I'm certain that careful scrutiny of the guests will lead us to the murder weapon, and therefore the killer."

POISONED PATISSERIE

It's not long past noon when you arrive at the pastry shop. Clemency Burnside, patissier by trade, has been found dead on the floor. Her three underlings greet you in a state of shock and introduce themselves as Ms. Ashe, Ms. Brooks, and Ms. Carter. They haven't called the police, afraid the shop would be closed down.

"The owner can always hire a new head baker," they explain, "but the shop wouldn't survive the scandal. We'd be out on the street!"

"Oh, I don't know," says Medea Thorne, shrugging. "Some people enjoy a bit of scandal with their morning croissant. But seeing as we're here . . . what exactly happened?"

"Convulsions she had," Brooks tells you. "It was horrible! She choked, and sort of gurgled, and collapsed. Grinning she was, which we've never seen her do. Before we knew what was happening, she was dead!"

"Risus sardonicus," Ms. Thorne nods. "Typical of tetanus, or strychnine poisoning. Do you know what she'd been eating?"

The women shake their heads. "We always have a sort of late breakfast together at eleven," says Ms. Carter. "And we all ate the same things. She might've had something at home?"

"It's unlikely, though, as she's usually on a diet," says Ms. Ashe. "She's always talking about how little she eats, but keeps sampling our cake icing all the time."

"Oh." Ms. Thorne shoots you a look. "And have any of the cakes been sold?"

"Not yet." The women explain that the cakes are meant to go out for delivery.

Ms. Thorne asks the women about each of the cakes and about themselves in excruciating detail, getting you to note it all down. Eventually, she asks them to make a round of sandwiches, coffee, and fresh éclairs.

"Do not eat or drink anything they give you," she instructs you. "I'm just off to ring Inspector Symes. Keep an eye on them. Particularly the perpetrator!"

Whom will you need to particularly keep an eye on?

Pictured, left to right:
GERALDINE ASHE: Pursued her dream to work in food despite a citrus allergy.
EREMINA BROOKS: Has a severe dairy intolerance, but loves patisserie.
CIBELLE CARTER: The most skilled, trained in Paris, and does all the
          fancy piping.

DAIRY-FREE VANILLA VELVET CAKE

VANILLA RAINBOW CAKE

MERINGUE CAKE
with just a hint of lime

ALMOND *and* ORANGE CREAM CAKE

WHITE CHOCOLATE BUTTERCREAM DREAM, *our bestseller*

LOW-FAT LEMON SURPRISE, *made without butter*

LAVENDER DELIGHT, *one for the connoisseurs*

BITTER COFFEE *and* CHOCOLATE CAKE *with* DARK FUDGE FROSTING

RASPBERRY MERINGUE CAKE

DEADLY PRESERVES

"You'll have read about the murder of Edgar McHugh?" Medea Thorne asks you in the car. "The wealthy shipping magnate? Rich as Croesus, and a miser, and frankly a terribly unpleasant man. No one can have been surprised that he's been poisoned," she adds rather ghoulishly. "The question really is why they haven't done it sooner."

"Who did do it?" you ask. "And how?"

"It seems there was poison in the jam," Ms. Thorne explains. "According to Inspector Symes, it was the last thing McHugh ate. He got up from the break-fast table, and collapsed. His cook confirms it was the first jar from a fresh batch they only got in yesterday. Gooseberry and Green Tomato, if you'll believe it. Homemade, artisanal stuff, you know, made by a lady called Ada Wildwood. Apparently, she's been supplying them for years."

Having passed a sign reading *Wildwood Homemade Jams and Preserves*, you arrive at your destination, a tumbledown house at the edge of a wood.

Symes greets both of you on the doorstep, and Ms. Thorne gets straight to the point. "Did she have any reason to murder him?"

"Not on the face of it," Symes rubs his chin. "According to the cook, McHugh and Wildwood had a falling-out, but that was years ago. McHugh was well known for his ferocious temper." He rings the bell. "The nephew gets the lot and would be the chief suspect, but he's in Kenya!"

The door is opened by a tall, gaunt woman who is looking quite unwell. Symes does all the talking, while she nervously looks you over, but she lets you in.

"That's quite a collection," Symes nods at the pots, ladles, and spoons hanging in the kitchen. "And a veritable apothecary!"

"Oh yes." She straightens her apron. "Many of my long-standing customers know that I like to experiment, so they bring me all sorts of implements and ingredients. Mr. Temperly next door always lets me have most of his elderberry harvest. Just the other day the vicar sent me palm sugar from Indonesia! And my friend Caroline Shayle came back from her cruise and brought me the most wonderfully ripe red ackee, as well as nutmeg and mace."

"You're friends with McHugh's secretary?" Symes narrows his eyes.

"Yes, in fact it was she who got me McHugh as a customer in the first place, all those years ago." She points at a framed photograph. "She used to mind his nephew, too. Even as a boy, young Ignatius loved to help me make jam. Now of course he's an anthropologist, always off in far-flung places, but he still writes to regale me with the most hair-raising stories. He sent me this lovely copper pan not too long ago, and this carved wooden spoon only last week. Pretty, isn't it?"

"Indeed," Ms. Thorne says grimly, turning to you. "I think it's obvious what's happened here, and which of these jams we'll need to confiscate . . . don't you?"

A DANGEROUS DINNER

"I'd love it if you came along, too," says Augustin Artaud, beaming at you. "It'll be quite the illustrious dinner."

"The guest list is spectacular," Medea Thorne agrees, studying a piece of paper. "But why on earth would you invite—hang on. Have you been through my files? Attempted murders that didn't come off?" She shakes her head. "This is a terrible idea. I'm fairly sure any of these people would be tempted . . . especially in this combination! You wouldn't want a brawl to break out. Or worse!"

"Well . . . " Artaud smirks deviously. "I did think it would add a certain frisson to the evening." He shrugs.

"Not on my watch," Ms. Thorne insists. "We'll just have to seat them in such a way that no one sits next to or opposite their archnemesis."

"If you like." Artaud obviously isn't bothered either way. "If you think it can even be done."

"'Course it can," Ms. Thorne scoffs, turning to you. "We're already late for an important claret tasting. Would you mind just sorting this out for me? Meet us at The Hesperides later."

As they swan off, you proceed to pull the necessary background information from the files, in order to devise a possible seating plan.

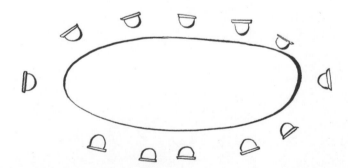

THEODORE RIDGE

Profession: Arctic explorer
Just returned from: Siberia
Famous for: Taming wild bears, vodka-snorting contests, the disappearance of a colleague near Spitsbergen, a touch of kleptomania, and his extensive vocabulary of colorful expletives. Denies having stolen some of the famous Cragspur pearls.

PERSEVERANCE CRAGSPUR

Profession: Deep-sea diver
Just returned from: Bermuda
Famous for: Retrieving many wrecks, wearing her most precious trinkets on her person at all times, being wanted by several states for concealment of treasure trove and various other small misdemeanors, a weakness for pearls, and lingering brackish scent.

EUNICE K. HENDERSON

Profession: Eminent psychologist, psychogeographer, and traveler of mental landscapes
Just returned from: The Painted Desert
Famous for: Her ability to move harp strings by sheer concentration, her collection of rare marbles, and her academic treatises on unsavory urges and strange inclinations. Indulged in a very public feud with Juliet Blears, who belittled her psychokinetic powers.

CLAYTON "SCORCHING" PERRY

Profession: Layabout and dashing man-about-town
Just returned from: The infernal regions
Famous for: Seven guidebooks to Hell and its immediate surroundings; unproven rumors of cannibalism; and a reputation as a prominent S&M enthusiast, orgiastic reveler, and competitive eater. A serial heartbreaker, he blithely jilts his lovers as soon as he tires of them, be they famous starlets, sportsmen, or supposed nobodies.

LOLA MAE WILLIARDS

Profession: Lunar explorer and television personality
Just returned from: The well-known ray crater Copernicus
Famous for: Being the first person to visit the far side of the moon; an extensive study of South Pole–Aitken basin; a predilection for silly jokes and reckless behavior; and her designs of the "moon stroller" lunar vehicle and "moon amble" roller skates. Unlucky in love and fiercely proud, she's known to hold a serious grudge.

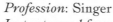

JULIET BLEARS

Profession: Singer
Just returned from: A concert tour spanning Kyrgyzstan, Uzbekistan, Turkmenistan, Kazakhstan, and Russia
Famous for: Being a former member of an occultist society, her dramatic moods, suffering for her art, her PhD in Russian literature, and a suspicion of all physicians, whom she has often publicly denounced as charlatans.

STEVEN MASTERSON

Profession: Former professional tennis player representing a well-known sportswear giant
Just returned from: His parents' house in the suburbs
Famous for: Mysteriously losing an arm, supposedly in a ballooning accident; publishing terrible poetry on the back of his tennis career; and wasting away due to heartbreak.

CLEMENTINE WHITE

Profession: Newspaper journalist and heiress to a gold-mining fortune
Just returned from: Bright Haven Rehabilitation Clinic
Famous for: Being an opium fiend, her acerbic wit, and her penchant for highly ornamental men. Made her professional name with sensationalist exposés on paranormal businesses that cash in on supposed hauntings.

AUGUSTIN ARTAUD

Profession: Ghost hunter
Just returned from: A friend's wedding in Beirut
Famous for: His smooth charm; his outrageous cocktail-mixing skills; and his extensive arsenal of the latest rayoscopes, thermographs, galvanometers, and other modern ghost-hunting equipment. Harbors an innate dislike of journalists, most of whom he'd brand as liars.

MARMADUKE ELLIS

Profession: Society photographer
Just returned from: His lawyer's office
Famous for: His keen nose for sniffing out scandal, supplying the major gossip rags with juicy details on everyone's life, and being universally unpopular with anyone of even vague public interest. Surprisingly, he's yet to have a run in with Ms. Thorne (or indeed yourself).

THE CRUCIVERBALIST CASE

"I've got too much on!" Inspector Symes moans. He's letting you into the flat of Percival Butcher, famously prolific setter of crosswords since retiring from professional boxing, and recently deceased at the hands of a person or persons unknown. "There are three other cases I need to get on to. We are painfully short-staffed. That's why I've asked you here."

"This is where he died?" Medea Thorne points at the desk.

"Yes. Butcher hardly ever left the apartment, so when he didn't answer the bell, his friend got so worried that he got a passing postman to help him force the door."

"Who is this friend?"

"Otis Gorge, a fellow puzzle enthusiast. He found Butcher dead at his desk. Heart failure. According to the people at his paper, he'd been calling in a panic, saying someone was changing the clues in his crossword to include death threats." Symes consults his notepad. "The first time the clues were changed to give *butcher*, *bloodshed*, and *revenge*. A few days later, it was *annihilation* and *shortly*. Yesterday, he said it was *demise*, *imminent*, and *tomorrow*. Of course, they all thought he was being over-dramatic. But now . . . "

"Yes, I see." Ms. Thorne surveys the room. "Has anything been touched?"

"Gorge says no, and the postman verified this. Of course, we'll get the whole place raked over as soon as possible." Symes sighs. "In the meantime, I thought you might cast your eyes over it. Was it murder? And how was it done?"

"There's an abundance of clues, indeed." Ms. Thorne nods, studying the crossword puzzle. "Yes. This is almost too easy." Extracting a pencil from her pocket, she circles several blank boxes in bright green. "There you have it. Come along, Symes, how about you treat us to some coffee while my assistant riddles this out. I could murder an espresso."

Who murdered Butcher, and how did he die?

ACROSS:

4. With 5-Across, a clean slate

5. See 4-Across

8. Cards with single pips

9. A disastrous outcome (informal)

10. Stinging plants

12. Nocturnal flying insects

14. Decay

15. Cruel, or animal-like

18. Insubstantial, otherworldly

19. Lacerations

20. Red or white bitter and poisonous fruits of low woodland plant

DOWN:

1. Long-necked wading bird, associated with the Egyptian god Thoth

2. Become dark as a result of burning, decay, or bruising

3. A dessert containing gelatin and cream, named after a region of Germany (like revenge best served cold)

4. With 16-Down, remnant of a travel receipt

6. Destroys utterly

7. Proficiency, skillfulness, cunning

11. First Aboriginal first class cricketer, 1848-1883

13. Criticize, or lament

16. See 4-Down

17. A hard felt hat with a rounded crown, or a famous horse race

19. Elegant

HALLOWEEN

Late one night, you are on your way to a Halloween soiree, having just interviewed a suspect at a nightclub in a deserted part of town. The rain is pelting down, and you're having trouble seeing through the windshield. Next to you, Medea Thorne is scanning the airwaves on the car radio, looking for spookier music, when you hear something almost like a scream.

"Did you hear that?" you ask, taken aback.

She merely shrugs. "I know. Shivers FM just isn't what it used to be."

Your headlights reveal something lying in the road. And there's something crouching over it, a red figure.

"Stop!" Ms. Thorne shouts, already unbuckling her seat belt as the car screeches to a halt.

The crouching figure has leapt up. Scrambling out of the car, you glimpse the figure disappearing into the huge, dark house looming to your right. Then you see the body. Illuminated by the glare of the headlights, the man lies unmoving on the wet tarmac, his vampire costume rapidly soaking full of blood.

"Follow that imp!" Ms. Thorne urges you. "Or devil, or whatever they're supposed to be. If you're quick they won't get very far."

You're already sprinting up the steps to the front door, which is still slightly ajar.

"Try to apprehend the suspect!" you hear Ms. Thorne calling.

Where is the suspect?

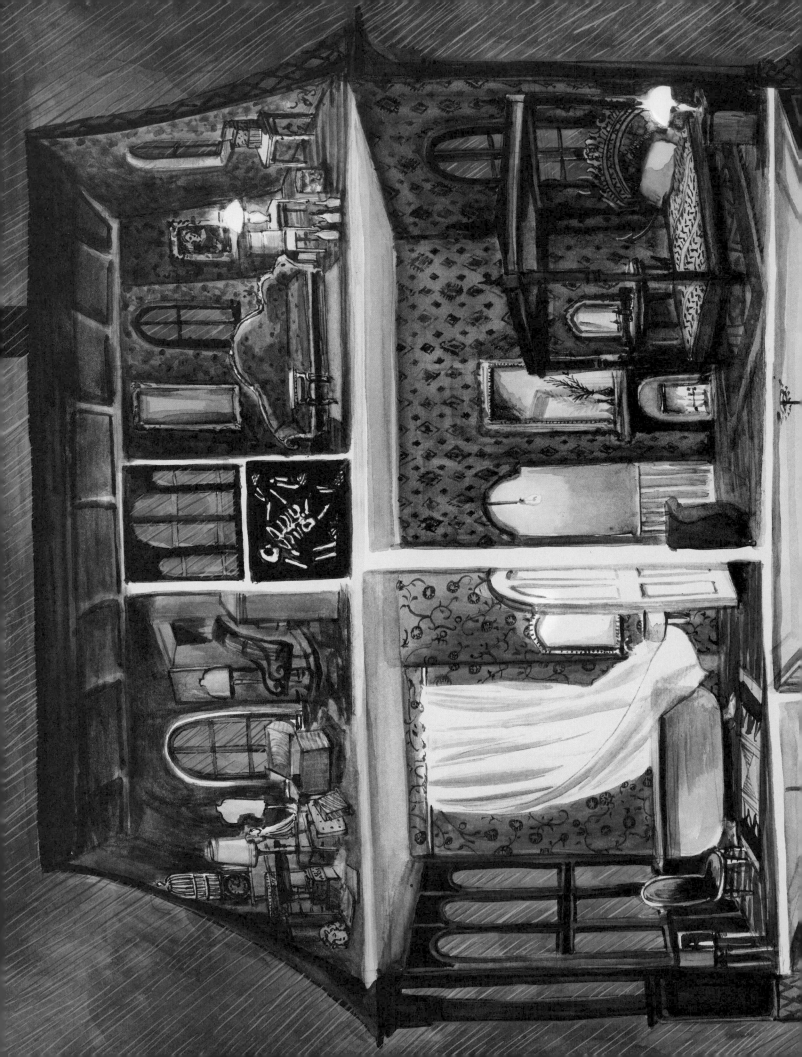

MURDER IN
THE LABORATORY

"Oh good, you're here." Medea Thorne greets you at the door. "We've been asked here by an old friend of mine, who's a—" she coughs a little, "a civil servant. Follow me."

As she leads the way through a labyrinth of corridors, she explains what happened.

"Dr. Nemo Blister. An eminent molecular physicist, part of a team of quantum chemists and atomic physicists. They're working on what I understand is a somewhat sensitive project." Ms. Thorne shoots you a look. "The cleaner found him earlier this evening. Coshed on the head. Your classic blunt instrument, I'm afraid."

You enter the laboratory. There's a strange smell in the air, possibly exuded by one of the countless gleaming instruments on every surface.

"This is his team." Ms. Thorne points out a large photograph on the wall. "Rivalry was rife among them, as well as a propensity for forming all sorts of amorous constellations, causing the inevitable fallout."

Having studied the photograph, you gingerly step up to the body on the floor. "That's a blunt instrument, all right."

Ms. Thorne nods darkly. "Well, he's obviously expected something to happen, because he's left us a clue . . . and an accurate one, I shouldn't wonder." She sighs. "I'll just take a few snapshots. Meanwhile, there's a telephone in the hall by the stairs. You'd best ring Inspector Symes and tell him whom to bring in for urgent questioning."

Pictured, bottom row to top, left to right:
FLORA LANCASTER, BOB CLARK, RUTH COOKSON,
VALERY WALKER, NICK RATHBONE, ALINA AMAR

$$\Sigma 1$$
$$=$$
$$\Delta_{6,7,8}$$
$$2$$
$$K \{0_x\}$$
$$M + e$$

28-6-19 | 88-90-5-8-10

THE
HUES
OF
LIFE
ARE
DULL
and
GREY
THE
SWEETS
OF
LIFE
INSIPID

HE A
BEWILDERED
ANSWER
GAVE

DROWNED
IN THE
SULLEN
MOANING
WAVE

LOST
IN THE
ECHOES
OF A
CAVE.

NEVER
ODD
OR
EVEN.

MURDER
FOR A
JAR OF
RUM

First
BURN A
BLUE OR
CRIMSON
LIGHT.
Then
SCRATCH
THE DOOR
AND WALLS.

THE MISSING WILL

"They're still deciding how Uncle Gregory died, whether it was murder or not. Personally, I suspect Aunt Ethelgilda, but I'm sure the police will work it out. In the meantime, we need to find that will!" Alasdair McGough paces the room. "He must've hidden it in the safe. I've emptied the desk, looked in the hidden drawers and behind the secret panels, but there's nothing of use. Not even a hint as to what the combination might be."

"I see." Medea Thorne scans the room. "Zoologist, was he?"

"Only an amateur," McGough says. "More money than sense. You know the type. Unlike his relatives, who, um," he clears his throat, "might be a lot more desperate for a pecuniary shot in the arm." He lets out a deep sigh. "If I don't get that safe open soon, I'll have to resort to explosives and blast a massive hole in it."

"That won't be necessary." Ms. Thorne smiles as she takes a seat on a little velvet sofa. "Everything we need is plain to see, and we'll most certainly help you. Especially as our fee obviously depends on it. How about you mix us a little drink and tell us all about these exotic beasts, while my assistant opens the safe for us."

What is the code?

Was it a bat I saw?

Mein Kopf ist ein Vogel.

And DARKLY FELL THE ANSWER DREAD — UPON THEIR UNSUSPECTING HEAD, LIKE HALF A HUNDREDWEIGHT OF LEAD.

THE MEADOWS BREATHING AMBER LIGHT THE DARKNESS TOPPLING FROM THE HEIGHT THE FEATHERY TRAIN OF GRANITE NIGHT.

LEARN FROM THE PIG TO TAKE WHATEVER FATE OR ELDER PERSONS HAVE HEAPED UPON YOUR PLATE.

LATE METAL

CANNOT PLEASURES, WHILE THEY LAST, BE ACTUAL- UNLESS, WHEN PAST THEY LEAVE US SHUDDERING, AND AGHAST WITH ANGUISH SMARTING? CANNOT FRIENDS BE FIRM & FAST AND YET BEAR PARTING?

Farewell Farewell my tea and Toast, my Meerschaum and Cigars!

THE CLAIRVOYANTS' CONVENTION

"This is a bit unusual," Inspector Symes begins uneasily, "but we need all the help we can get. I know you don't hold with this mumbo jumbo. That's why I feel certain you can help us sort the wheat from the chaff, so to speak."

"What's actually happened?" Medea Thorne blinks in the sunlight, looking suspiciously pale. "Fortune tellers, did you say?"

"A whole international convention of them!" Symes shakes his head. "One of their number's been strangled in the bathroom."

"Didn't the victim see it coming?" Ms. Thorne smirks, raising an eyebrow.

"You're not the first person to point that out, Ms. Thorne. Think of the repercussions if this came out. Naturally, the venue as well as the organizers are trying to keep this under wraps." He clears his throat. "We haven't alarmed anyone yet, and we haven't let anyone leave. But we've established that the victim was going to expose one of the exhibitors as a scam artist, an impostor. We need to track that person down before anything else happens. The question is, which of them is phony?"

"Aren't they all . . . ?" you begin, but Ms. Thorne cuts you off.

"Excellent," she beams, turning to face you. "I'm going out for a smoke. Go on ahead, have a good look around. I'll join you in a minute, but I'm sure by then you'll be able to tell us who did it."

Let's talk NUMEROLOGY
INTRIGUES
INFIDELITIES
SUCCESSIONS TO ESTATES
YOUR ENEMIES' SECRETS
BETTING TIPS
MOST ACCURATE ORACLE
WILL TELL YOU WHAT YOU WANT TO KNOW
TEMPLE OF KNOWLEDGE
INTERNATIONAL SPIRIT BOARDS
ROBOT FROM THE FUTURE
DISPENSES LOVE ADVICE
CONSULT THE BLACK MIRROR
ASK THE WAX
CERTIFIED CEROMANCERS
EGYPTIAN SCRYER
YOUR DESTINY REVEALED
SIGHTS
DR. CROCODILE THE DIVINER
WILL CAST RUNES, SHELLS, BONES, CRABS
YOUR FUTURE
YOUR PAST
EVERYTHING BIBLIOMANCY
ASK ME YES OR NO

GROUNDS FOR SPECULATION
FINEST CHINA TEA & TURKISH COFFEE
READING INCLUDED WITH EVERY CUP
FIRST CHOICE
PALMIST
LOVE
LUCKY CHAN'S
SUPERIOR FORTUNE CONFECTIONS
ALL KNOWING PARROT
GIVES NAMES of FRIENDS and ENEMIES
CRYSTAL GAZER TO THE
BUSINESS WARNINGS
FINANCIAL FORECASTS
INVESTMENT ADVICE
LOTTERY NUMBERS
PRIVATE CONSULTATION

THE EXPLORER RETURNS

You're walking along a quay in the cargo port when Medea Thorne suddenly calls out, "Inspector Symes!"

Across the road, the inspector stops dead outside the Black Cat Café and looks up in surprise. He hesitates for an instant before waving you over.

"This is fortuitous," he says grimly. "I'm just about to meet Havilland Macmillan, the famous explorer. She's only just arrived on the Blue Star Line, having spent six months in Papua New Guinea. Her husband Henry died two days ago, found dead in their flat by the cleaner. He was lying at the foot of the stairs with a broken neck."

"Accidental death, then?"

"You'd think so! Only the top step had been smeared with engine grease to make sure he would slip. Someone's attempted to wipe it away as well, but it's left a very definite stain. It was murder."

Ms. Thorne nods slowly. "Who would have a motive for killing him? Apart from the wife, that is?"

"No one." Symes frowns. "He was very well liked. She inherits the lot! And I understand he wouldn't grant her the divorce she wanted . . . his death is a real result for her." He sighs. "But with an alibi like that—she's just stepped off the boat! There's no way she could have done it."

"Isn't there?" Ms. Thorne gives you a shrewd look, before turning to Symes. "You won't mind if we take a quick look at the grieving widow's possessions while you console her?"

Once inside the café, you encounter the formidable Ms. Havilland Macmillan. Posing as officers of the Harbor Police Pest Control unit, you and Ms. Thorne gain access to the explorer's two surprisingly compact trunks.

"Nothing in this one." Ms. Thorne dismisses the one containing clothing. "This one, however . . . " Having laid out the contents of the second trunk, she studies the many items for about a minute.

"Ah. Yes." She claps you on the back, murmuring quietly, "See, she could've easily done it! This proves it. You explain it all to Symes when he's done with the woman. I'll go and get us a stiff drink."

How can you prove that Macmillan may well have done it?

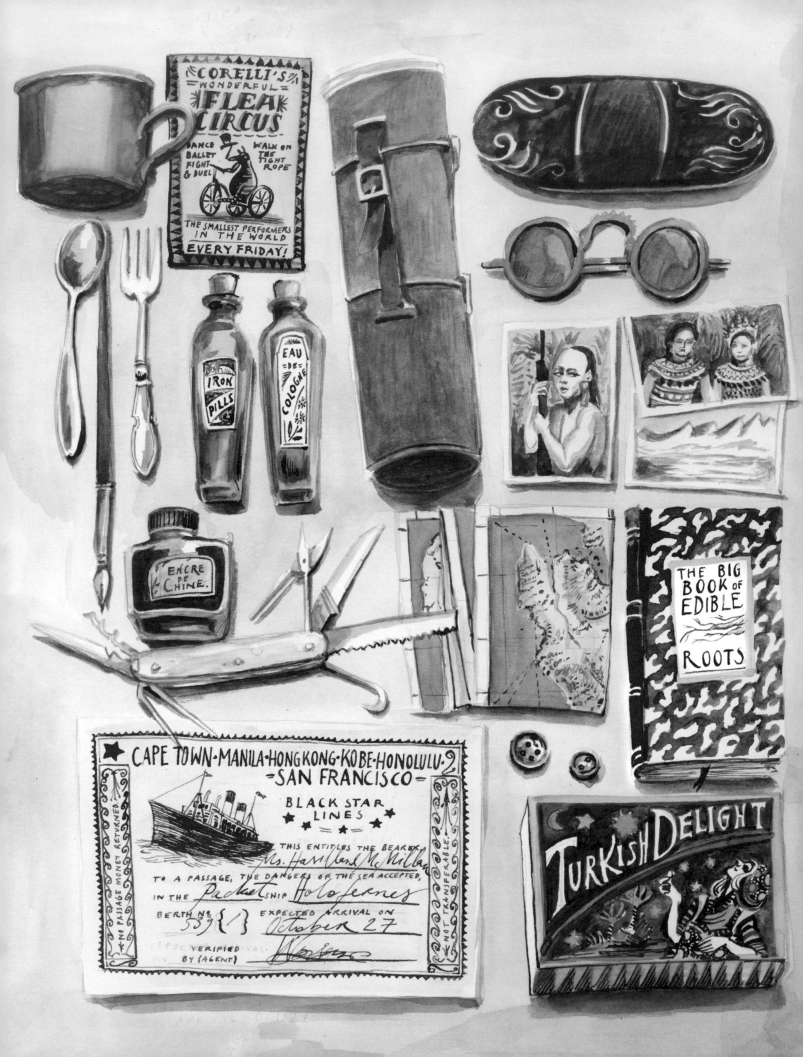

CLUES

THE COLLECTOR
Look out for a pattern! Then find what's missing.

PICKLED DELIGHTS
Something is missing from the display of pickles.
Where can it have gone without leaving a trace?

THE BOATING LAKE
They are snazzy dressers. Best investigate their outfits closely.

THE CHOCOLATE BOX
Incriminating items are strewn around the living room.

THE HESPERIDES
Be sure to look at both illustrations, and you'll find them!

SWEET DEATH
The colors of the shelves tell you which sets belong together within
puzzles, with brass plaques indicating each separate puzzle. These
are straightforward number puzzles: add, subtract, multiply across
shelves, sometimes diagonally. Some of the numbers might be digits of
a bigger number. Some are simple sequences. Don't be intimidated!

THE TOPIARY GARDEN
Try to spot a pattern. One tree doesn't fit.

THE FUNERAL PARTY
What might the weapon be? One of the suspects was
more able to access it than the others.

SERIAL MURDER
There is a theme to the items found at each of the six
murder scenes. One of the items is very specific.

A HAUNTING
Lots of red herrings, but it's just a matter of proving
the motive . . . check in the bedroom!

DEATH IN THE FOUNTAIN
Which one costume has the capacity to inflict this
particular wound inconspicuously?

POISONED PATISSERIE
Take into account the manner of death and the suspects' various allergies.

DEADLY PRESERVES
In the absence of any traceable toxic ingredients in the jam itself,
we must assume the poison came from something else.

A DANGEROUS DINNER
You and Ms. Thorne may have to act as buffers.

THE CRUCIVERBALIST CASE
The most obvious thing may not be the solution at all.

HALLOWEEN
Look for horns and a tail!

MURDER IN THE LABORATORY
It's a classic rebus puzzle. Say it out loud! Then think atomic numbers.

THE MISSING WILL
The code is hidden on the wall, not just to be read quietly.

THE CLAIRVOYANTS' CONVENTION
Look closely at the animals.

THE EXPLORER RETURNS
Do the dates add up?

SOLUTIONS

THE COLLECTOR

If you work out what is missing, you'll know which of them did it. There are two of each kind of thing in the cabinet of curiosities, but one pair is incomplete. The missing item is an Egyptian piece, a statue of Anubis, of particular interest to one of the suspects: Gregory Ramsbottom.

PICKLED DELIGHTS

One serving implement is missing: a large ladle for beetroot pickled eggs, the murder weapon. Because of the suspects' outfits, only Winifred Raybourne can have secreted the thing away on her person. It's too big for the pocket of a pair of shorts or a clutch bag. And it would've visibly stained any pale clothing.

THE BOATING LAKE

If you look closely, you can spot the murder implements hidden in the patterned clothing of all five suspects: a butcher's knife in Carlisle's jacket, a sword hidden in the pattern of Partridge's coat (below the oar), another sword hidden near O'Brien's collar, a knife near Garnett's right shoulder, and a sabre hidden in Ribbons's head-dress. As it turns out, they all did it together.

THE CHOCOLATE BOX

The following clues can be located in Mrs. Blake's flat:

> Evidence of financial troubles
> A packet of oleander seeds
> A mortar and pestle
> Two boxes of syringes
> Rubber gloves in the waste bin
> A tweed suit among the shawls and dresses in the wardrobe
> Fake mustaches
> A bit of ribbon from a chocolate box
> A receipt from The Chasm
> Betting slips
> A bottle of crème de menthe

THE HESPERIDES

SWEET DEATH

Each group of jars is a number puzzle in which a missing number can be worked out. Once you eliminate the eight solutions, the remaining jar, 21, is the one the poisoner tampered with.

I.   In each group of four, the bottom left number × top right number = top left and bottom right numbers read as digits. 7 × 6 = 42, therefore the missing number is 4.

II. This is simply a sequence of the numbers 1 to 6 squared: 1^2, 2^2, 3^2, ?, 5^2, 6^2. The missing number is 4^2, and 4 × 4 is of course 16.

III. The number in the center is the difference between the numbers on either side. The missing numbers are 7 and 5.

IV. If you read the jars as digits, the pattern is top shelf – middle shelf = bottom shelf. 97 – 38 = 59. The missing digit is 9.

V.   Fiendishly, there is no particular pattern here, it's just the numbers 1 to 15. The missing number is 12.

VI. Multiply the sum of the top number and the bottom left number by the bottom right number and you get the number in the center. (? + 7) × 5 = 75 The missing number is 8.

VII. In this sequence, the differences between the numbers are 9, 14, 19, 24; i.e., it increases by 5 at every step. The missing number is 96.

VIII. As in the previous puzzle, the difference between two consecutive numbers keeps increasing at a steady rate, in this case by consecutive prime numbers:
1 (+3) 4 (+7) 11 (+11) 22 (+13) 35 (+17) 52. The missing number is 35.

THE TOPIARY GARDEN

The trees have been planted in a pattern. Each row and each column contains each of the six styles of topiary—much like a Sudoku puzzle. But one tree is wrong. That's where the body is buried. The tree in question is the third tree from the right in the third row from the bottom.

THE FUNERAL PARTY

The sharp spear from one of the ice sculptures is missing. The murderer broke off the tip and used it to stab the victim. The only person tall enough to reach the spear on that sculpture is Enrico Mallow, the perfumer.

SERIAL MURDER

In each photo you can spot at least one of these objects:

    An empty box frame
    Small paper envelopes
    Tweezers
    Pins
    A jam jar
    A bottle of ethyl acetate
    A small net
    A magnifying glass

From these clues, you can surmise that SLBF stands for the Society of Lepidopterists and Butterfly Fanciers.

A HAUNTING

From his luggage we can see that Parker is planning to take a painting with him, which suspiciously matches the shape of a painting missing from the bedroom wall! We can safely assume that purloining this valuable item was his motive for killing Ms. Morengo. He might have staged the ghostly effects to muddy the evidence and explain his own rapid departure.

DEATH IN THE FOUNTAIN

The killer wears a hatpin—the murder weapon—and their clothes suggest a struggle near the ink fountain.

POISONED PATISSERIE

You can work out who prepared each cake based on the bakers' allergies and skills:

Dairy-Free Vanilla Velvet Cake–
any of them

Meringue Cake, with just a hint of lime–
Carter (fancy piping)

*Vanilla Rainbow Cake–*any of them

Lavender Delight, one for the connoisseurs–
any of them

*White Chocolate Buttercream Dream, our bestseller–*Ashe or Carter (contains dairy)

Low-Fat Lemon Surprise, made without butter–
Brooks or Carter (citrus)

Raspberry Meringue Cake–
Carter (fancy piping)

*Bitter Coffee and Chocolate Cake with Dark Fudge Frosting–*Carter (fancy piping)

Almond and Orange Cream Cake–
Carter (citrus and dairy)

Strychnine is a bitter poison, so it must be in the chocolate cake, which would mask the flavor.

DEADLY PRESERVES

It was the nephew who instigated his uncle's murder from afar, by sending the special carved spoon. We can assume that it is made of poisonous wood, such as ouabain, or the poison arrow tree. We can see that Ms. Wildwood has been cooking up a batch of yellow turmeric jam, but it might be safer to confiscate everything she's produced since she started using the toxic spoon.

A DANGEROUS DINNER

Avoid seating these people together or opposite one another:

RIDGE / CRAGSPUR
(He may have stolen her pearls.)

HENDERSON / BLEARS
(Public feud.)

MASTERSON / PERRY
(Masterson is still pining for Perry, who may well have had something to do with the loss of his arm.)

WILLIARDS / PERRY
(They have a travel writer's rivalry, and he may have ditched her.)

WHITE / ARTAUD
(He dislikes journalists, and she keeps publicly bringing his profession into disrepute.)

ELLIS / EVERYONE!
(He's got dirt on them all! You and Ms. Thorne must sit on either side of him.)

One possible seating arrangement would be:

THORNE *(at the head of the table)* –
ARTAUD – HENDERSON –
WILLIARDS – WHITE – BLEARS –
MASTERSON – CRAGSPUR – PERRY –
RIDGE – YOU – ELLIS.

THE CRUCIVERBALIST CASE

The crossword solutions are:

ACROSS:

4. and 5. Tabula Rasa;
8. Aces; 9. Curtains;
10. Nettles; 12. Moths;
14. Rot; 15. Beastly;
18. Ethereal; 19. Cuts;
20. Baneberries.

DOWN:

1. Ibis; 2. Blacken;
3. Bavarois;
4. and 16. Ticket stub;
6. Annihilates; 7. Art;
11. Twopenny; 13. Deplore;
17. Derby; 19. Chic.

When you solve the crossword, you can see the phrase "It's under your nose." The murderer's crossword antics were intended to shock Butcher into using the smelling salts. The old label on the bottle of smelling salts reveals that it really contains the poison prussic acid, or hydrogen cyanide.

HALLOWEEN

The murderer is hiding behind the headboard.

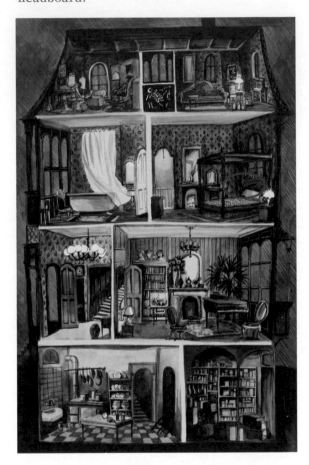

MURDER IN THE LABORATORY

On the blackboard, the solution is written out as a rebus, i.e. a pictogram puzzle, in which the symbols are used purely for their sounds, regardless of their meaning. In classic rebus style, if part of a word is to be ignored, the numbers representing the position of the unnecessary letters are shown as crossed out. Thus, △ ("triangle") minus the 5th, 6th, and 7th letters, becomes "trian."

It can therefore be deciphered as sum one is trian(gle) to k (n)il me, that is, "Someone is trying to kill me."

The numbers on the right-hand side are atomic numbers from the periodic table. Match the number to the corresponding letter(s) on the table to spell the murderer's name: Ni C K | Ra Th B O Ne.

THE MISSING WILL

The combination is in the framed words: "Oh, force heaven nigh! No fort to free," which are homonyms for numbers: 04790423.

THE CLAIRVOYANTS' CONVENTION

The impostor is using a trained monkey to find out personal details as well as stealing client's possessions.

THE EXPLORER RETURNS

The calendar in the hall where the dead body lies indicates the day he died was Saturday, October 26. The boat ticket is for October 27. The advertisement for the flea circus says it occurs "every Friday," and the flea-circus ticket stub confirms Macmillan was there on October 25. She had a motive, and we now know she also had ample opportunity.

ACKNOWLEDGMENTS

I would like to thank my brilliant editor, Mirabelle, for her faith and hard work and great patience; Kayla for indulging my design foibles; and everyone else at Chronicle who helped make this happen!

Thank you also to Felix, Bill, Jenny, Jon, Eren, Clemens, Lina, and Barbara for your input and sage advice. I'm indebted to my nearest and dearest for putting up with me while this thing was in the works. Above all, thank you Chris for your incredible support throughout this project! It's meant everything.